MALCOLM'S MARTIANS: EX

The Brain Terrain: When Lightning Strikes

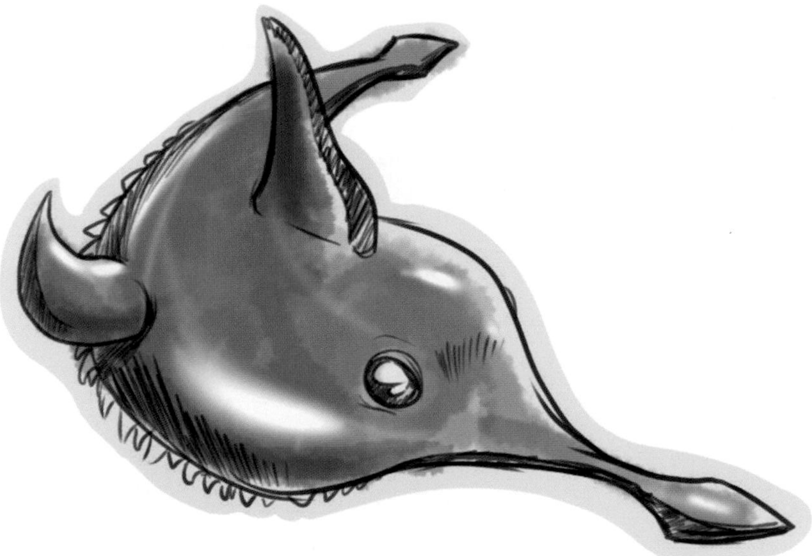

by Jason M. Burns

illustrated by Dustin Evans

Published in the United States of America by Cherry Lake Publishing Group
Ann Arbor, Michigan
www.cherrylakepublishing.com

Reading Adviser: Beth Walker Gambro, MS, Ed., Reading Consultant, Yorkville, IL

Book Designer: Book Buddy Media

Torch Graphic Press is an imprint of Cherry Lake Publishing Group.

Library of Congress Cataloging-in-Publication Data has been filed and is available at catalog.loc.gov

Cherry Lake Publishing Group would like to acknowledge the work of the Partnership for 21st Century Learning, a Network of Battelle for Kids. Please visit http://www.battelleforkids.org/networks/p21 for more information.

Printed in the United States of America
Corporate Graphics

TABLE OF CONTENTS

Mission log: August 10, 2055.

Today, we are visiting a place called the brain terrain. I don't know what it is, but it sure sounds awesome. I can't wait to see what it looks like so I can start drawing the Martians that live there. Dad says it will be unlike anything we have seen so far. My friend, Daniela, barely slept a wink last night because she is so excited. Best vacation ever!

—Malcolm Thomas

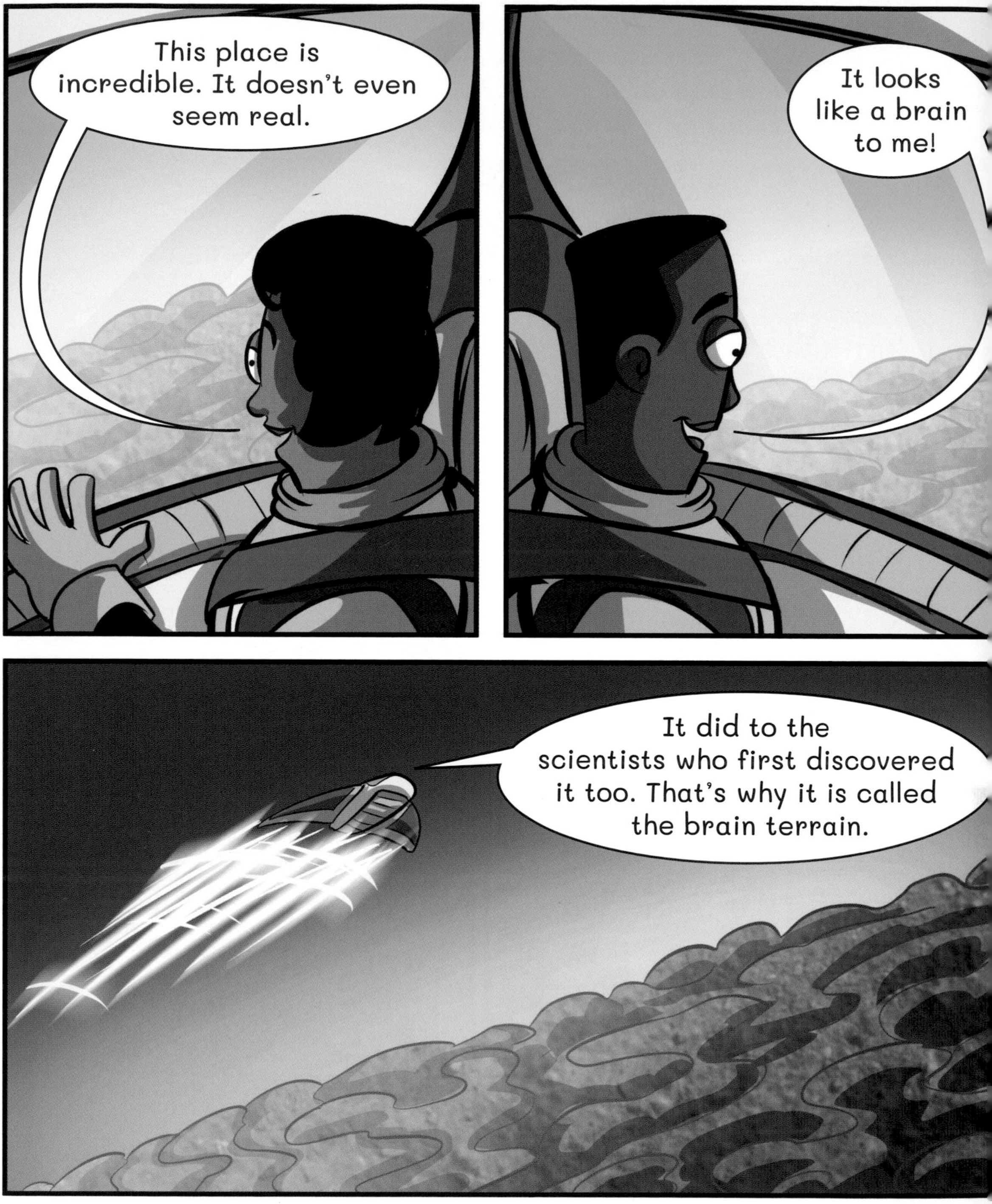
This place is incredible. It doesn't even seem real.
It looks like a brain to me!
It did to the scientists who first discovered it too. That's why it is called the brain terrain.

MARS FACT

The brain terrain is found in the middle latitude regions. These are zones located just north and south of a planet's equator.

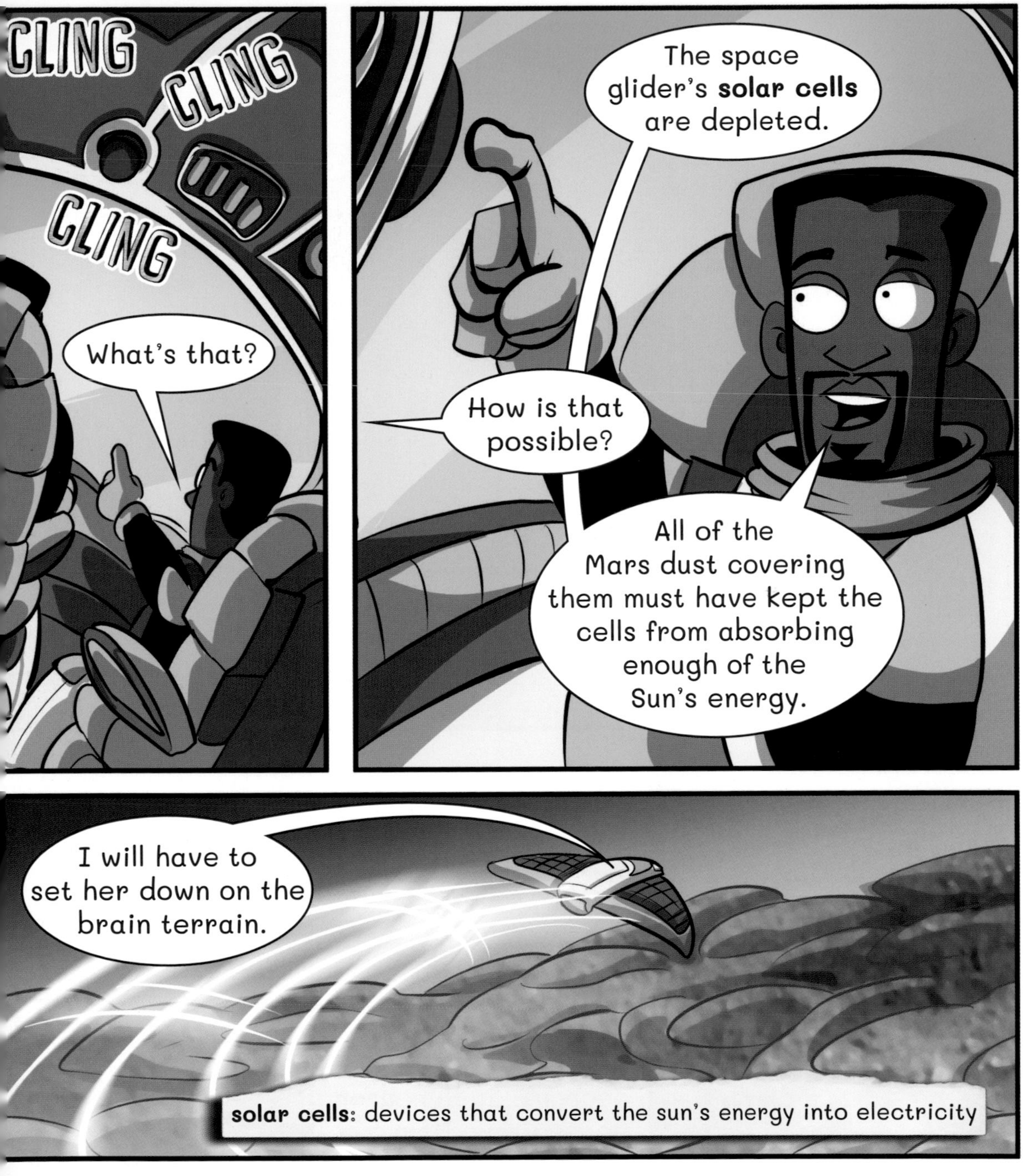
CLING
CLING
CLING
What's that?
The space glider's **solar cells** are depleted.
How is that possible?
All of the Mars dust covering them must have kept the cells from absorbing enough of the Sun's energy.
I will have to set her down on the brain terrain.

solar cells: devices that convert the sun's energy into electricity

MARS FACT

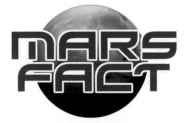

The brain terrain is mostly a mystery. Scientists believe the series of ridges and channels may have been formed by ice that exists beneath the surface.

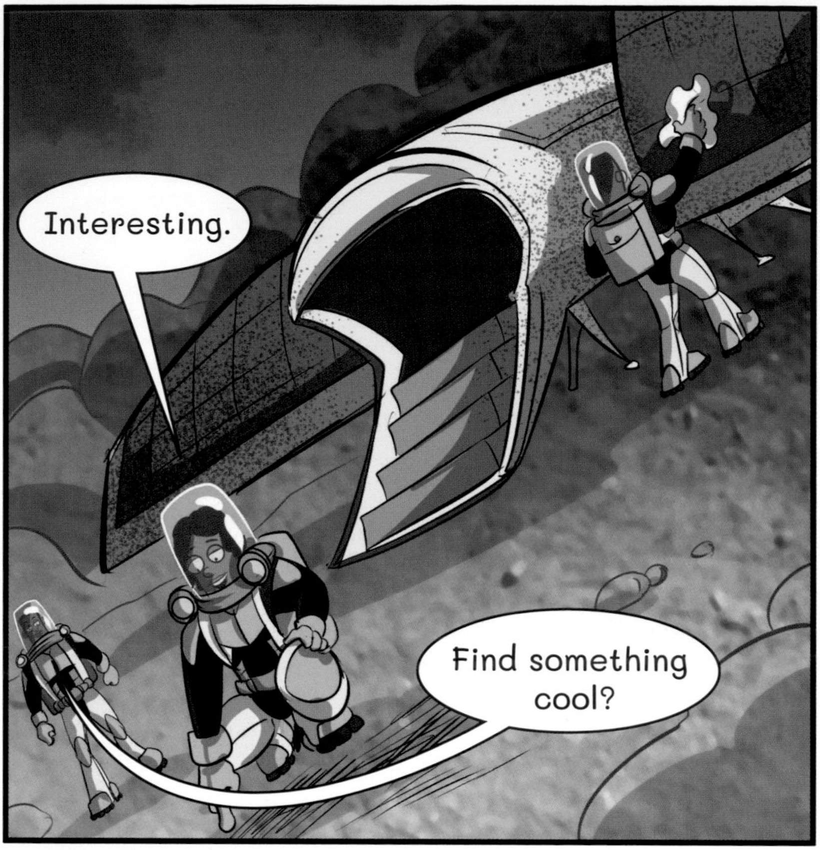
Interesting.
Find something cool?

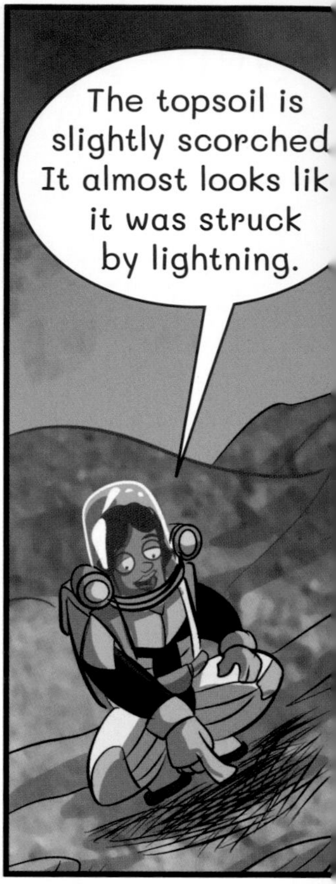
The topsoil is slightly scorched It almost looks lik it was struck by lightning.

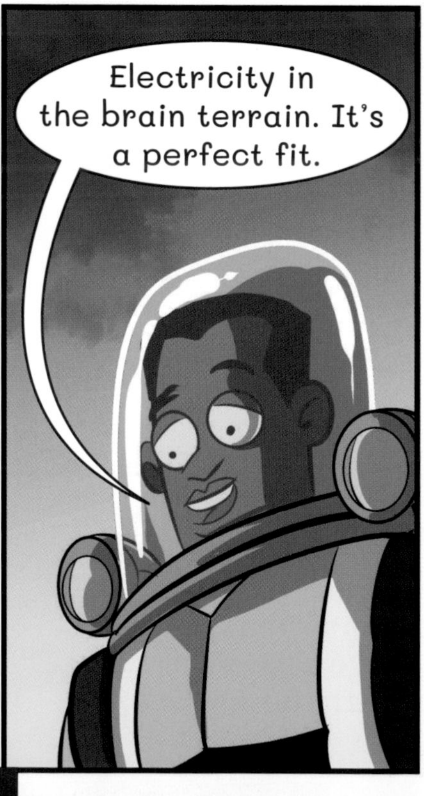
Electricity in the brain terrain. It's a perfect fit.

SCIENCE FACT

The human brain contains billions of cells called neurons. Each neuron generates a tiny amount of electricity. Your brain makes enough electricity to power a light bulb.

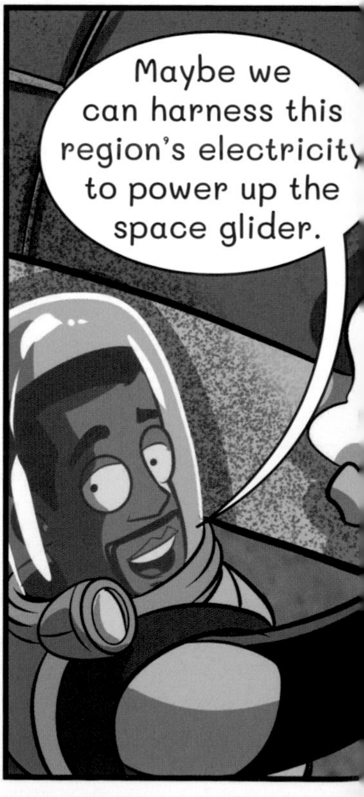
Maybe we can harness this region's electricit to power up the space glider.

THE CASE FOR SPACE

Lightning is a common sight on Earth, but does it strike as frequently on Mars? The planets have very different **atmospheres**. Mars has much lower air pressure than Earth. How does that affect lightning strikes?

• Scientists first detected lightning on Mars in 2009.

• Additional evidence of lightning was difficult to come by. Scientists wanted to know why.

• Sand storms are frequent events on Mars. Experiments were held to see what kind of lightning was generated by sand storms.

• An electric charge is created when the sand particles bounce off of each other. This is called the triboelectric effect. It means that electricity is caused by contact.

• Static electricity is a kind of triboelectric effect.

• The experiment showed that it was difficult to generate electricity at low air pressure. This means that lightning on Mars would be much weaker than it is on Earth.

• Lightning can exist on Mars. It is just less common.

atmospheres: layers of gas that surround planets

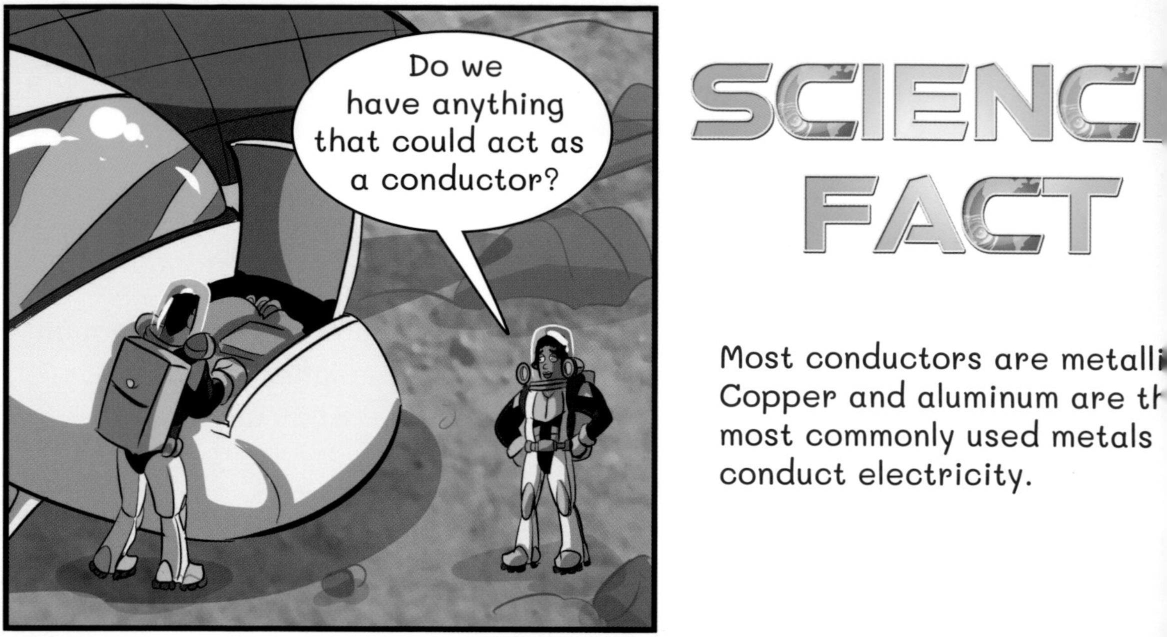
Do we have anything that could act as a conductor?

SCIENC FACT

Most conductors are metalli Copper and aluminum are tl most commonly used metals conduct electricity.

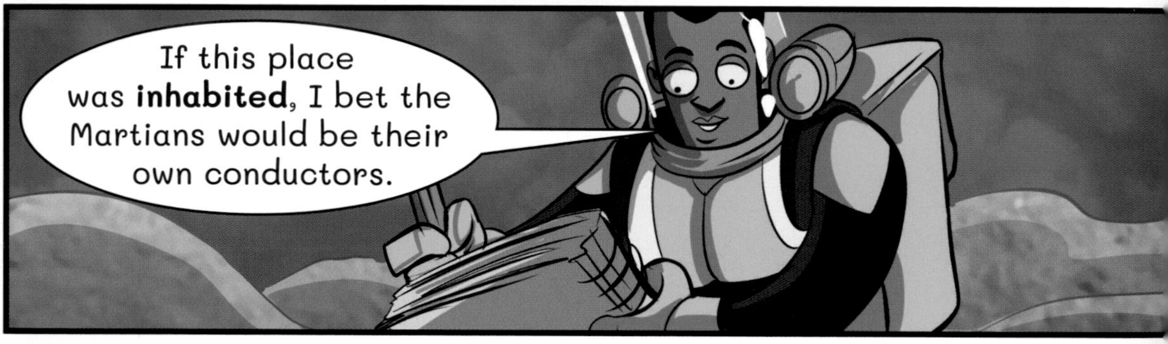
If this place was **inhabited**, I bet the Martians would be their own conductors.

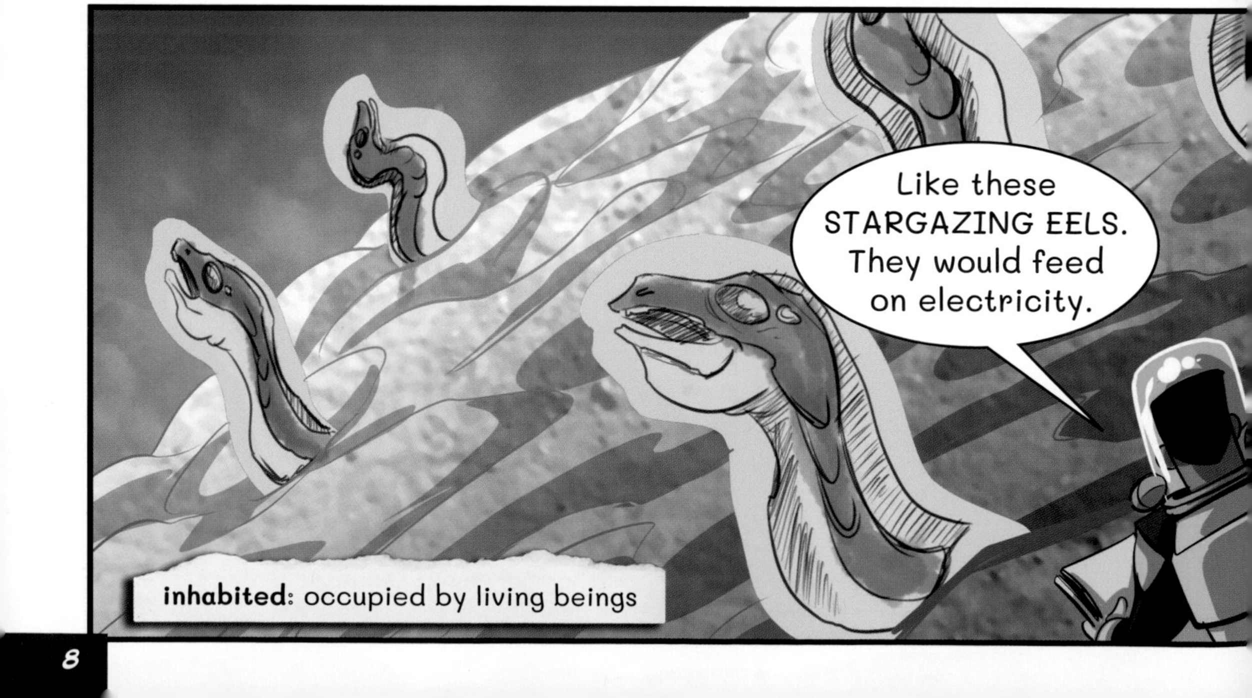
Like these STARGAZING EELS. They would feed on electricity.

inhabited: occupied by living beings

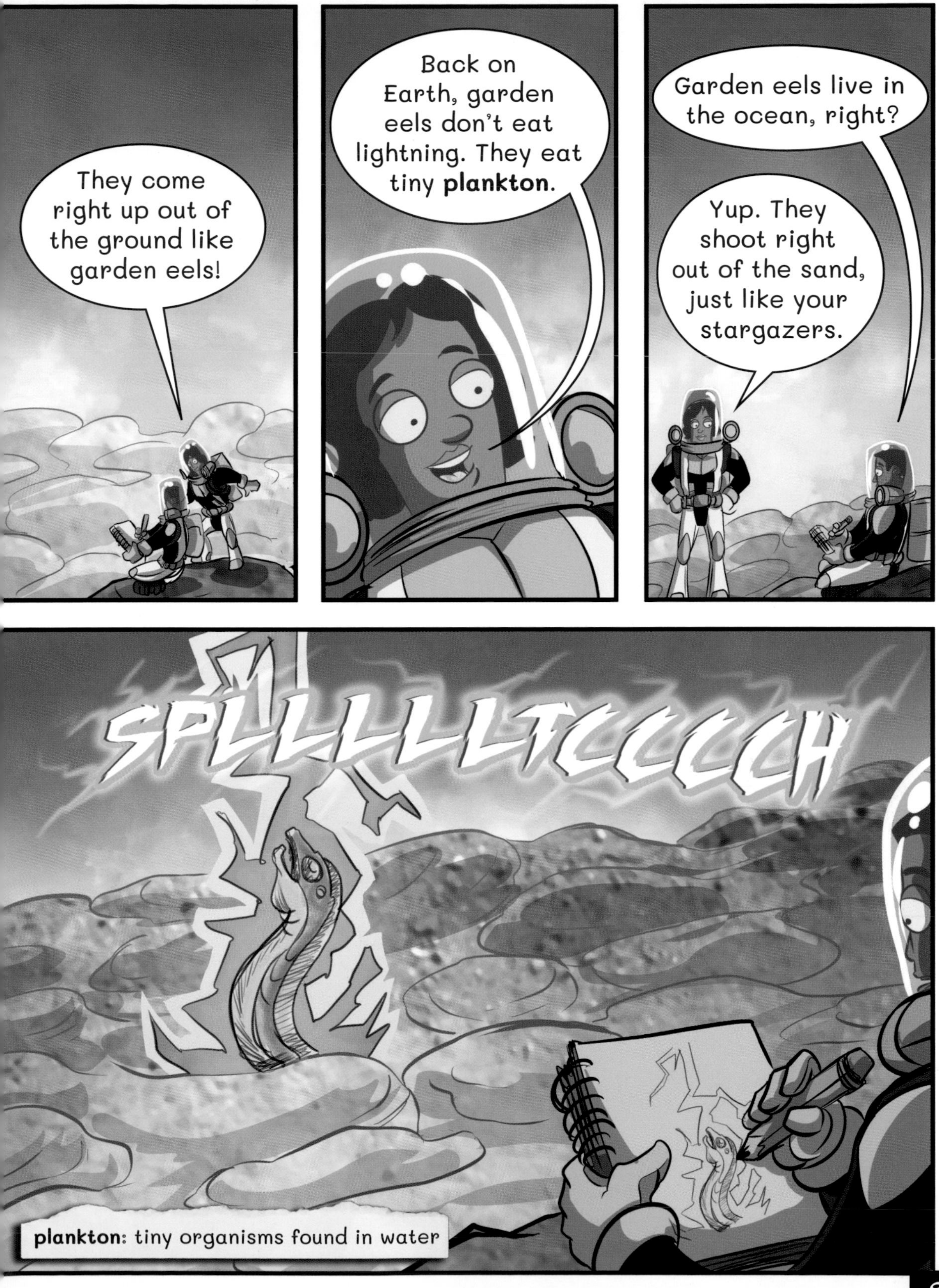
They come right up out of the ground like garden eels!
Back on Earth, garden eels don't eat lightning. They eat tiny **plankton**.
Garden eels live in the ocean, right?
Yup. They shoot right out of the sand, just like your stargazers.
SPLLLLLTCCCCH
plankton: tiny organisms found in water

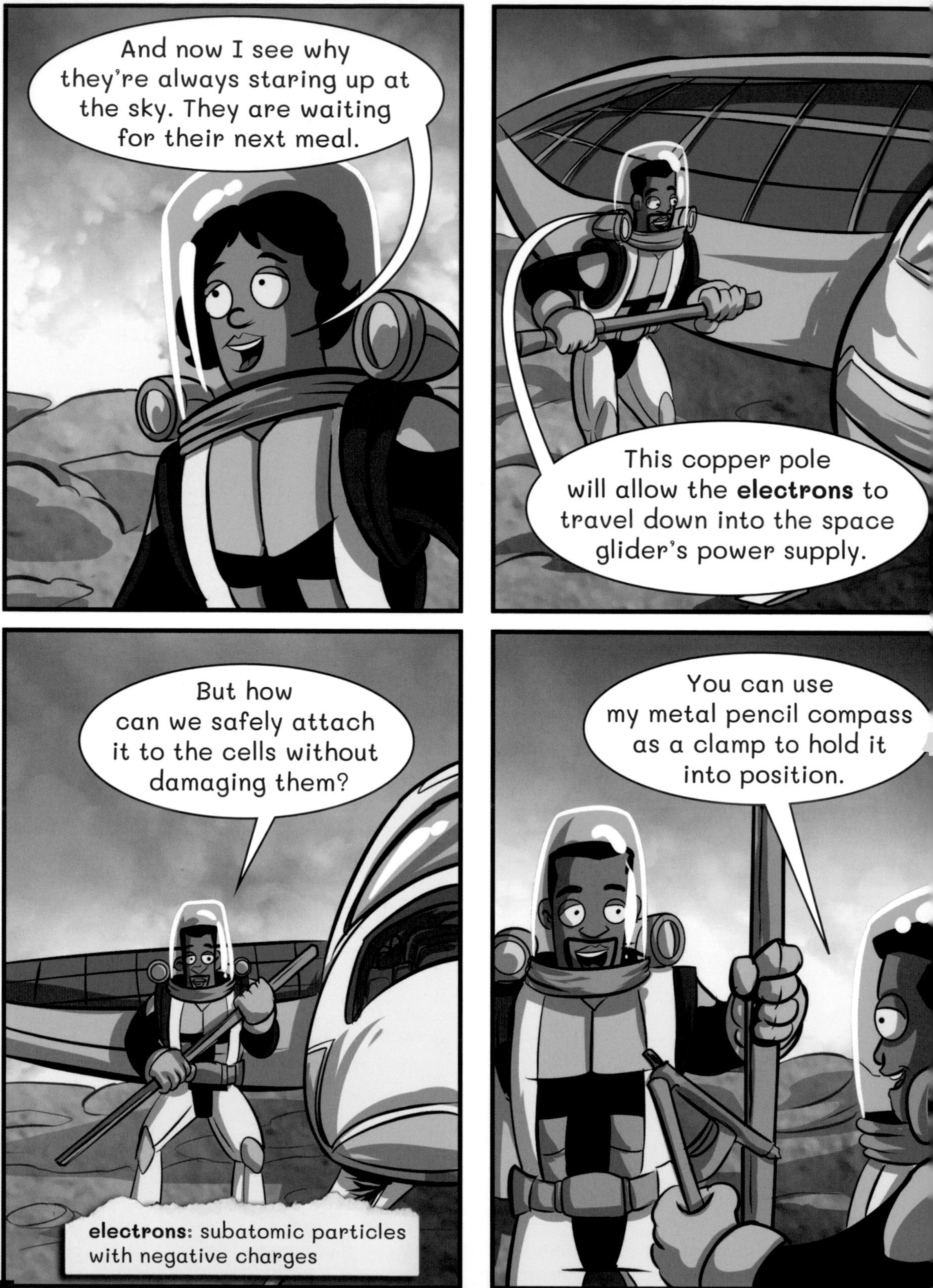
And now I see why they're always staring up at the sky. They are waiting for their next meal.
This copper pole will allow the **electrons** to travel down into the space glider's power supply.
But how can we safely attach it to the cells without damaging them?
You can use my metal pencil compass as a clamp to hold it into position.

electrons: subatomic particles with negative charges

THE SCIENCE OF SCIENCE FICTION

Some houses have solar panels. Did you know that spacecraft do as well? Solar energy is extremely important to space missions, especially those within Earth's orbit. Let's shine a light on the subject and see how it's used!

•Solar power is energy created by the Sun. Solar panels absorb energy from the Sun. The energy causes electricity to flow.

•Satellites that orbit Earth use solar energy because they are close to the Sun.

•The farther away the object is from the Sun, the less effective solar energy becomes.

•Solar energy is also used to power Mars rovers.

•Because Mars is millions of miles farther away from the Sun, the rovers require bigger and more sophisticated solar panels.

•NASA's spacecraft *Juno* is orbiting Jupiter. It was the first solar-powered space probe.

•*Juno* is equipped with 3 solar panels. Each one measures 30 feet (9 meters) long.

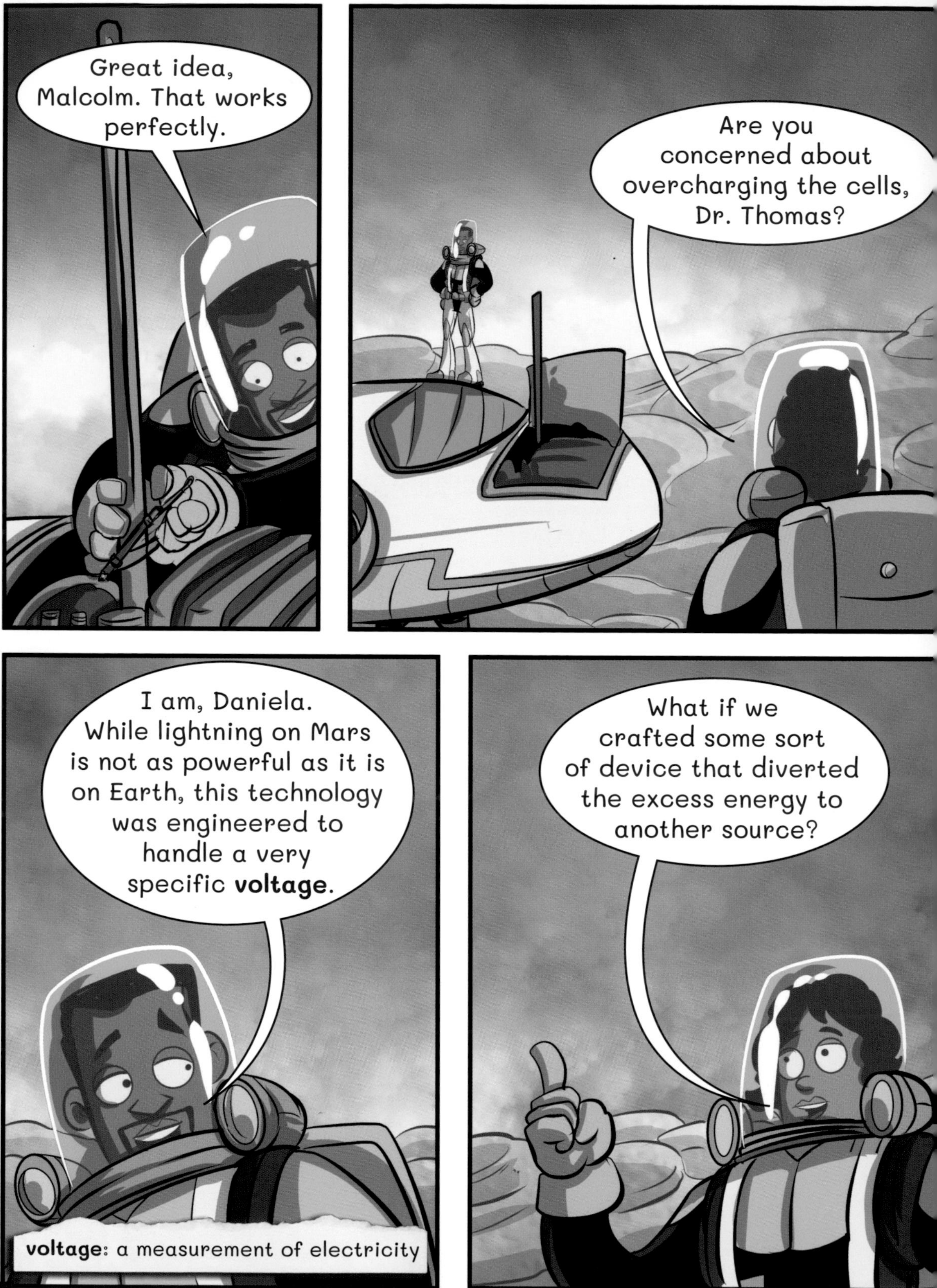
Great idea, Malcolm. That works perfectly.
Are you concerned about overcharging the cells, Dr. Thomas?
I am, Daniela. While lightning on Mars is not as powerful as it is on Earth, this technology was engineered to handle a very specific **voltage**.
What if we crafted some sort of device that diverted the excess energy to another source?
voltage: a measurement of electricity

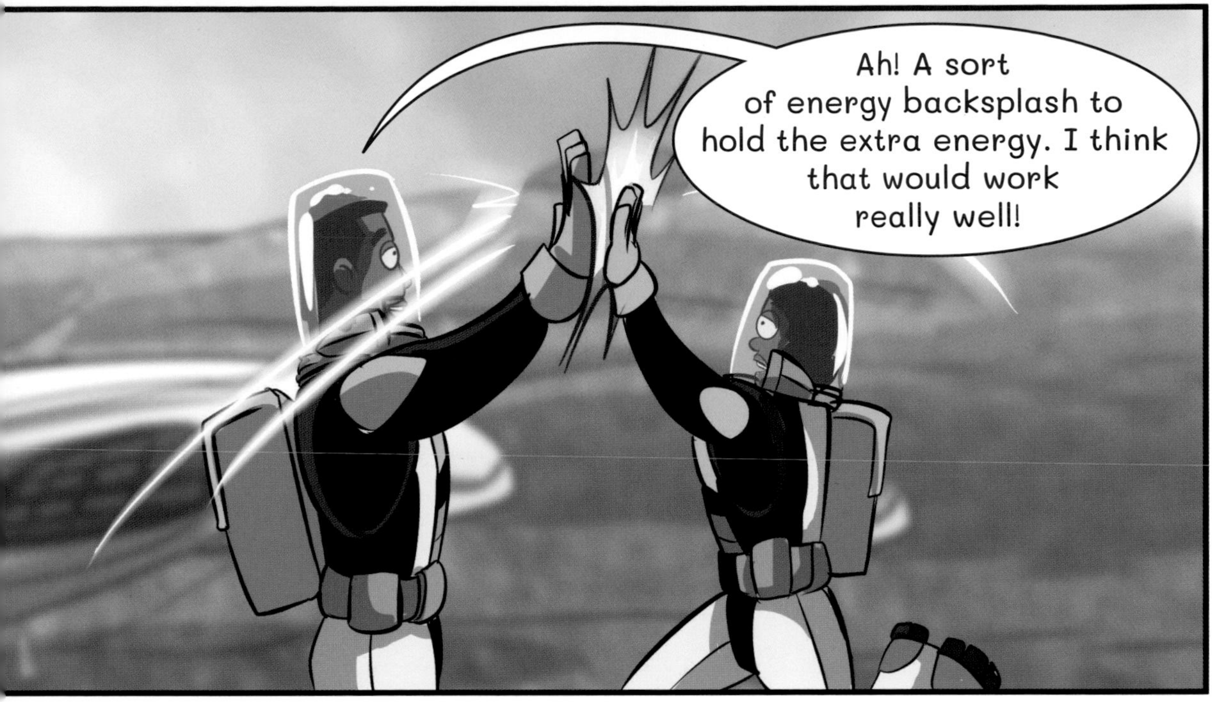
Ah! A sort of energy backsplash to hold the extra energy. I think that would work really well!

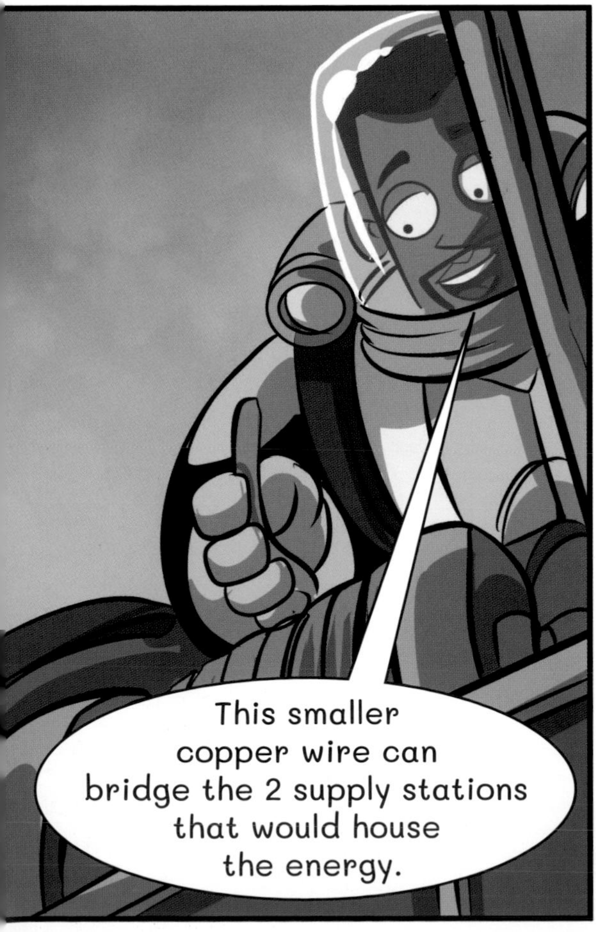
This smaller copper wire can bridge the 2 supply stations that would house the energy.

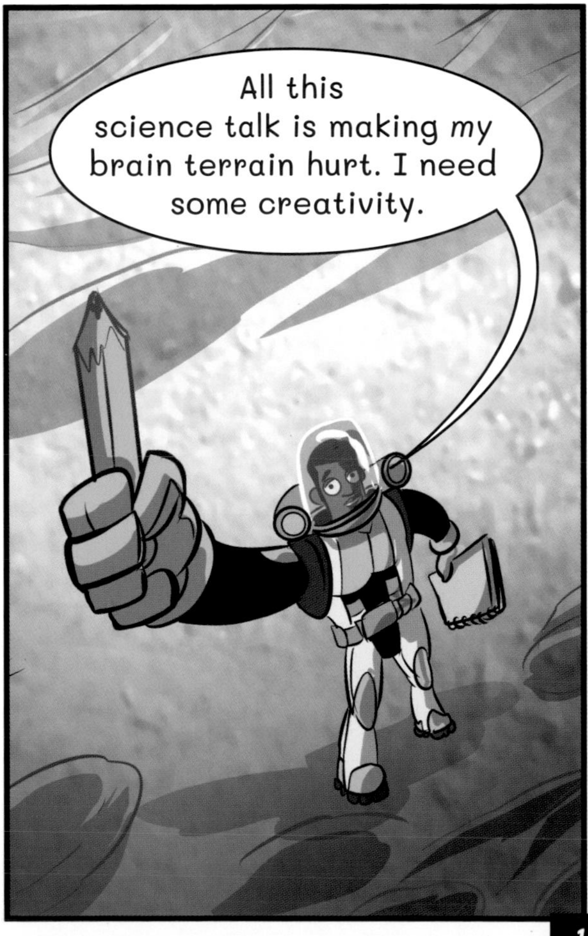
All this science talk is making *my* brain terrain hurt. I need some creativity.

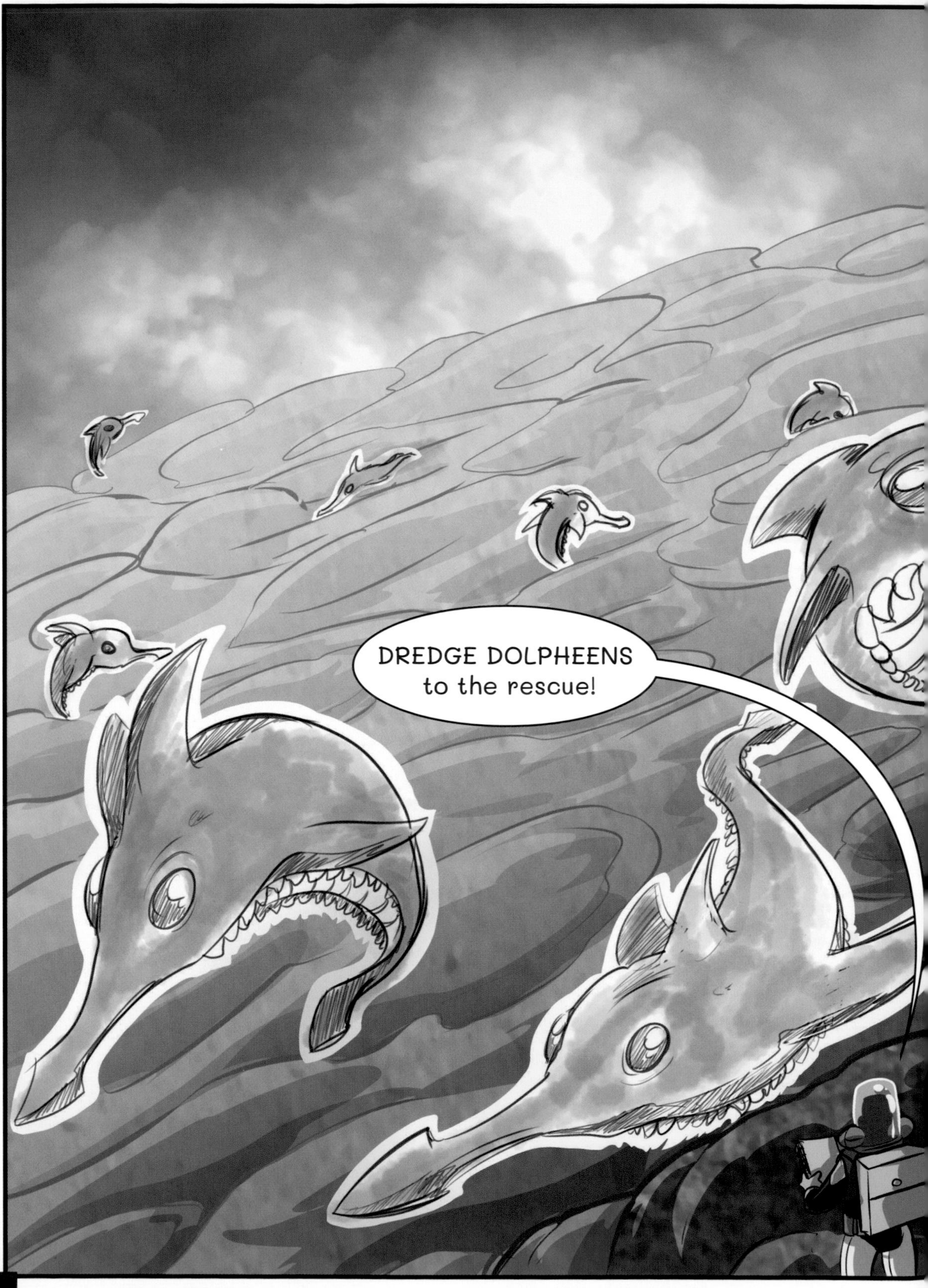
DREDGE DOLPHEENS
to the rescue!

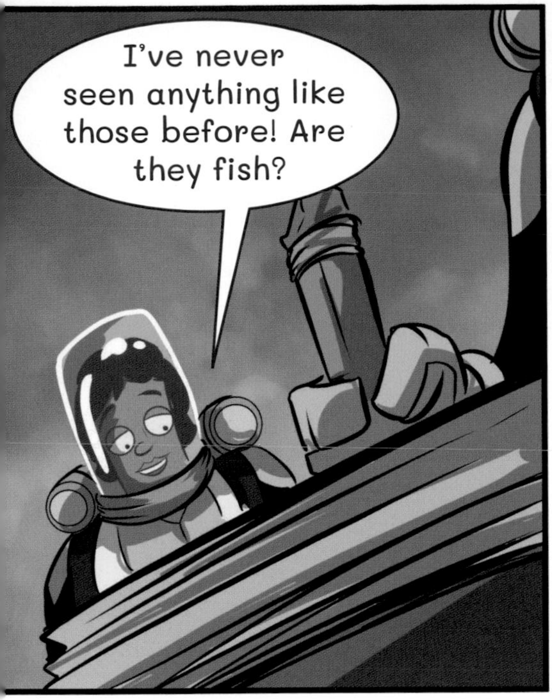
I've never seen anything like those before! Are they fish?

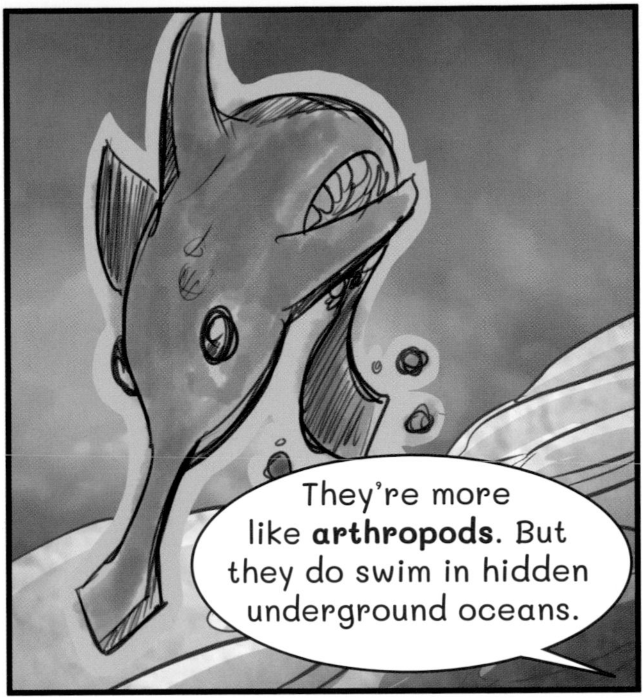
They're more like **arthropods**. But they do swim in hidden underground oceans.

MARS FACT

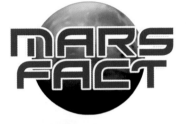

Scientists have discovered multiple bodies of water beneath the surface of Mars. They believe they are saltwater lakes that are both frozen and liquid.

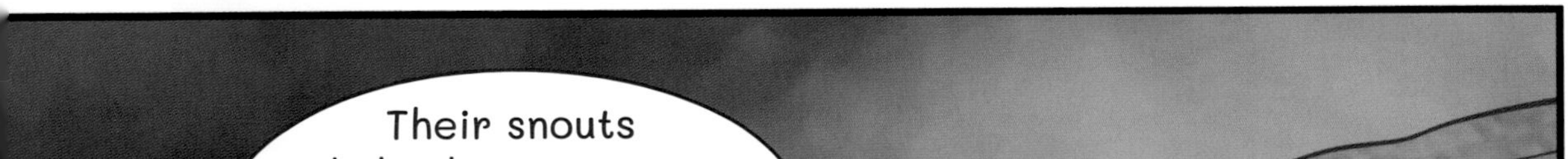
Their snouts help them emerge out of the brain terrain and then go back in again.

arthropods: invertebrates with jointed body parts, such as spiders, insects, and crustaceans

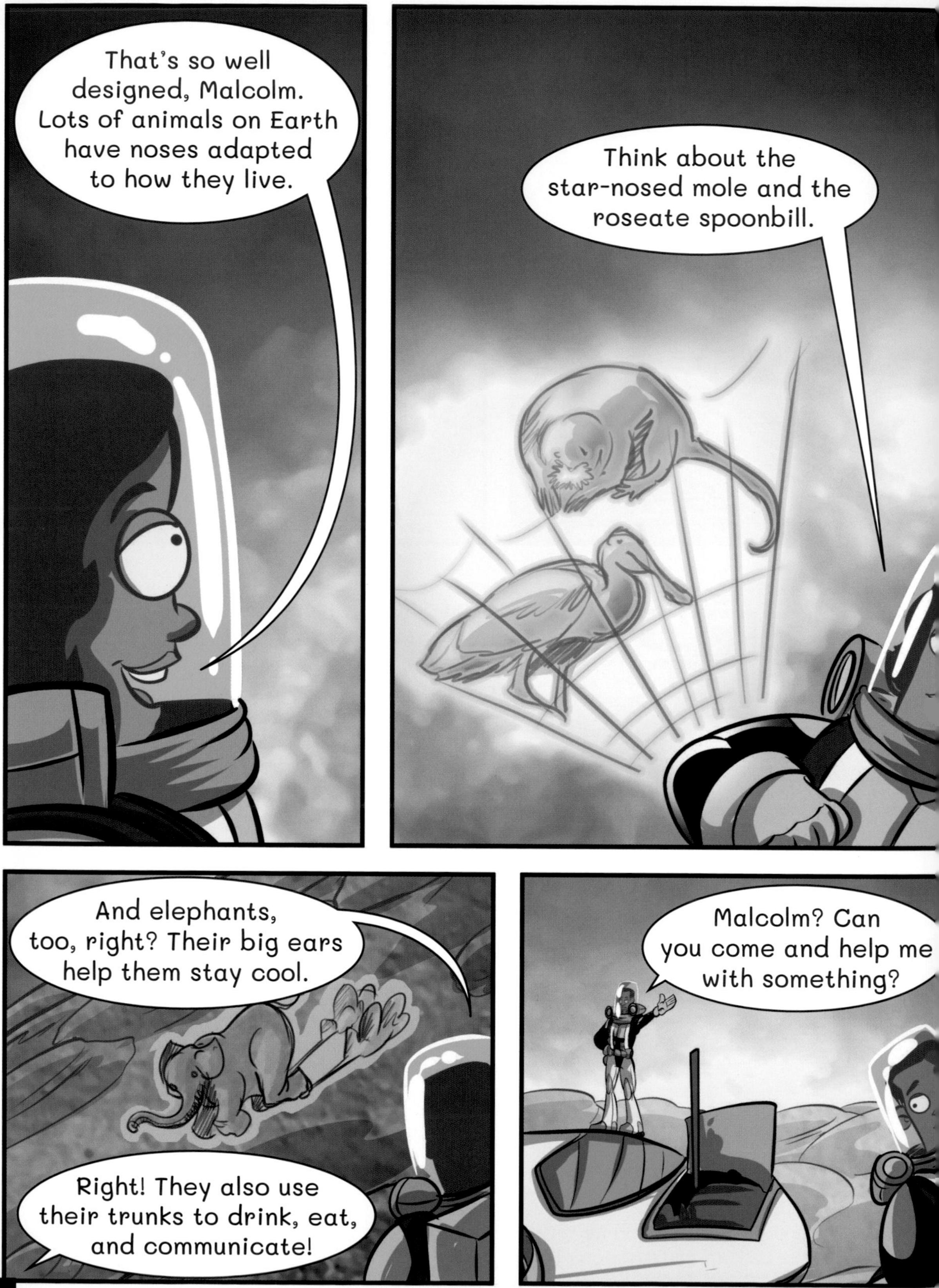
That's so well designed, Malcolm. Lots of animals on Earth have noses adapted to how they live.
Think about the star-nosed mole and the roseate spoonbill.
And elephants, too, right? Their big ears help them stay cool.
Right! They also use their trunks to drink, eat, and communicate!
Malcolm? Can you come and help me with something?

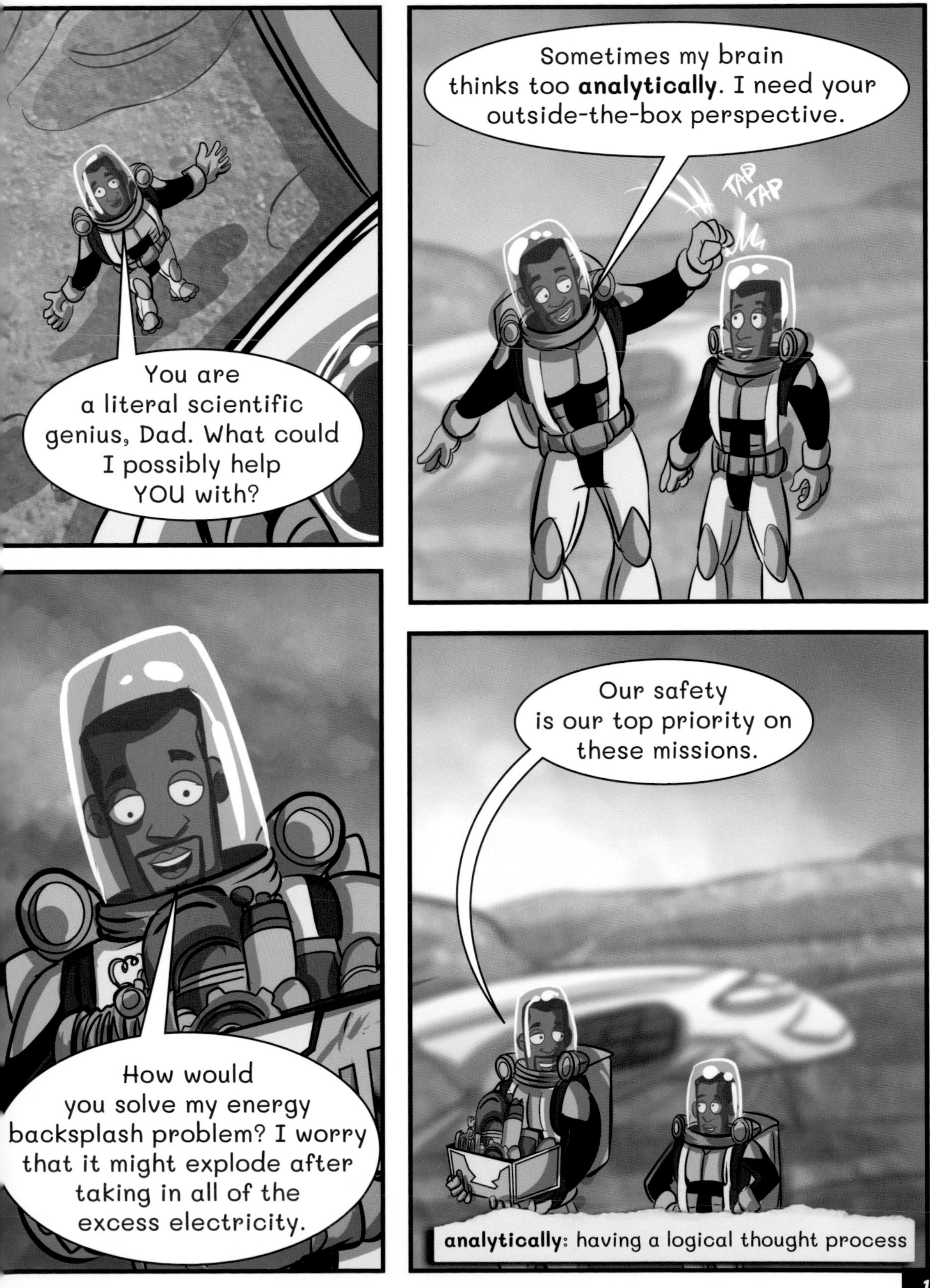
You are a literal scientific genius, Dad. What could I possibly help YOU with?
Sometimes my brain thinks too **analytically**. I need your outside-the-box perspective.
TAP TAP
How would you solve my energy backsplash problem? I worry that it might explode after taking in all of the excess electricity.
Our safety is our top priority on these missions.
analytically: having a logical thought process

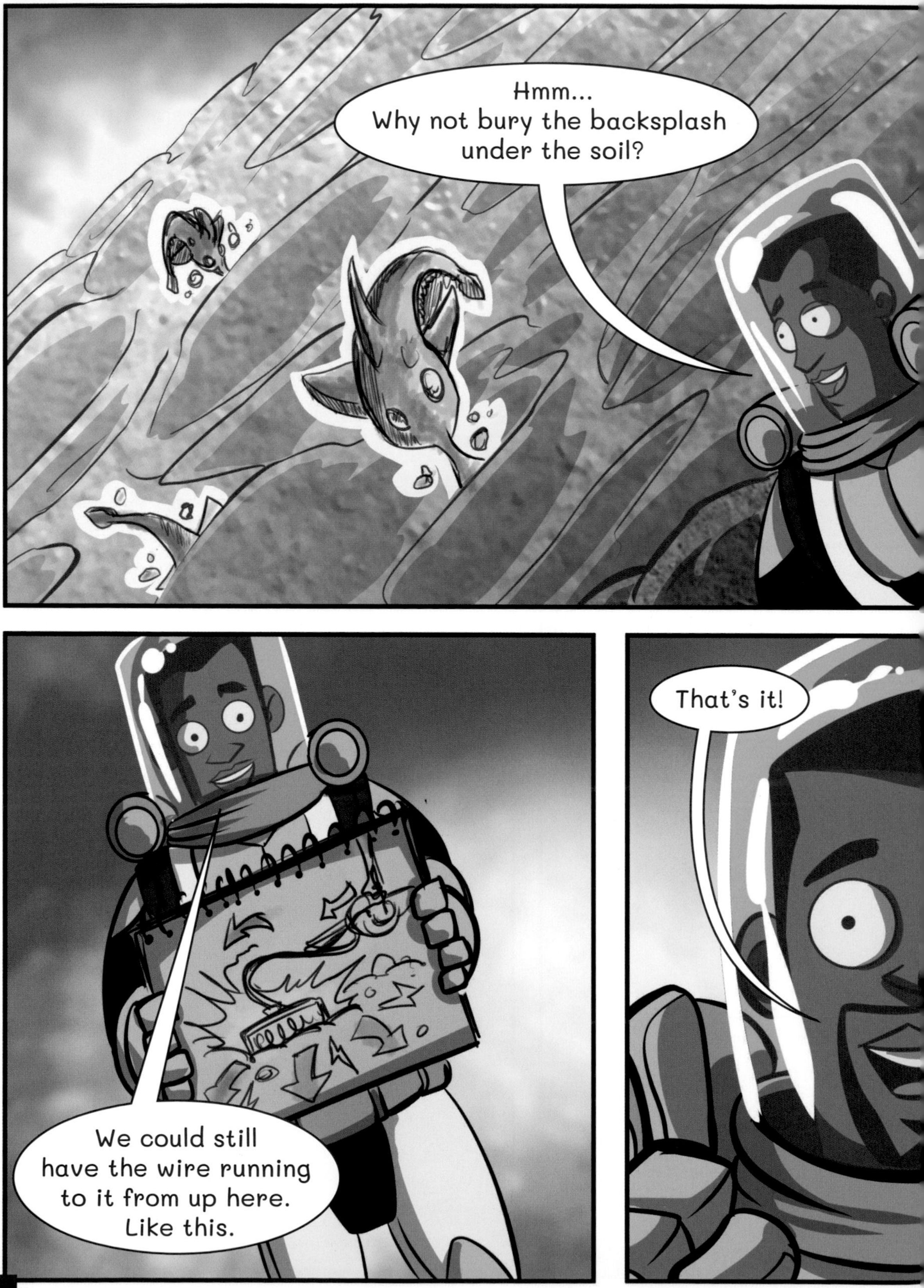
Hmm...
Why not bury the backsplash under the soil?
We could still have the wire running to it from up here. Like this.
That's it!

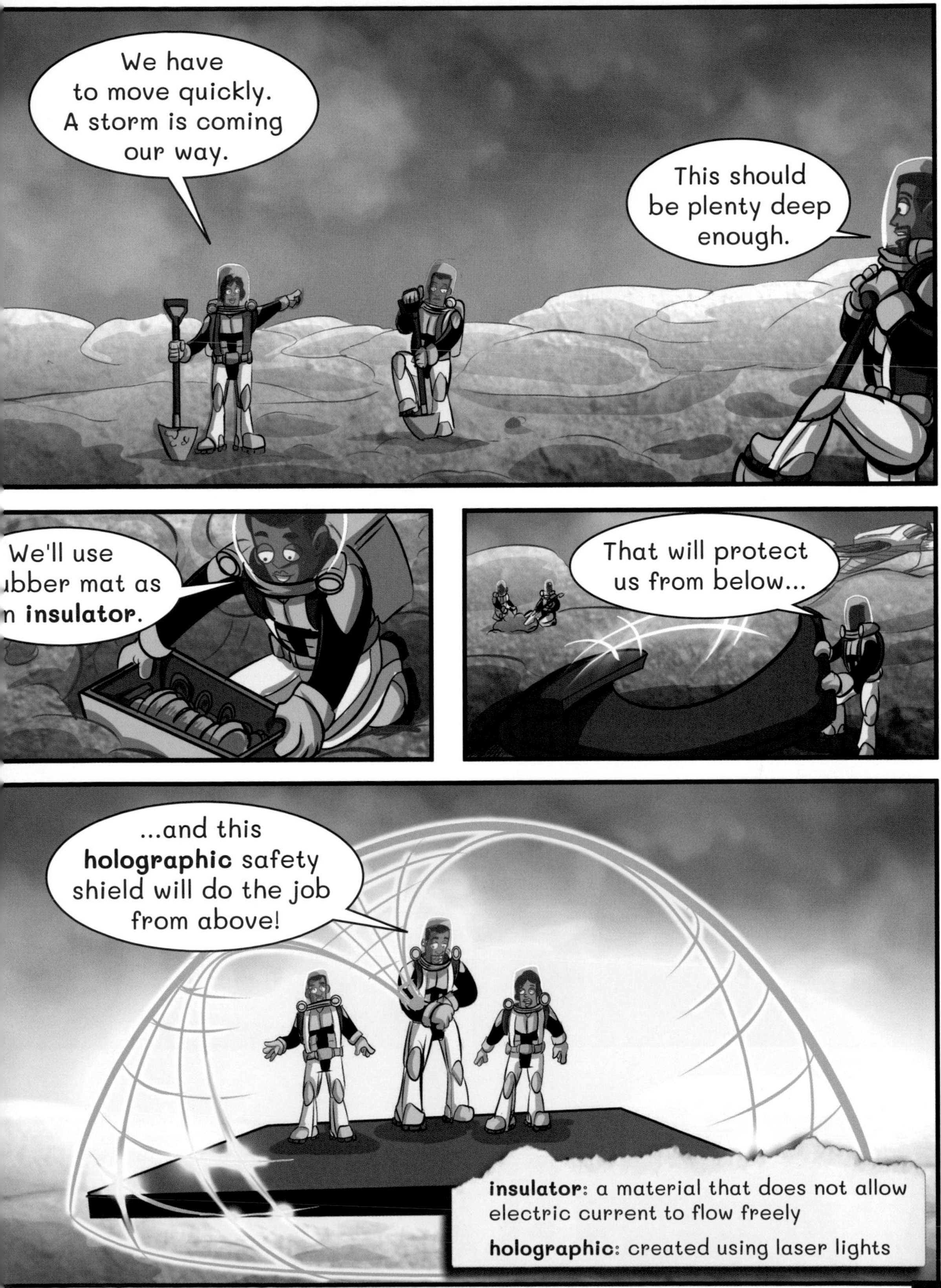

We have to move quickly. A storm is coming our way.
This should be plenty deep enough.
We'll use
ubber mat as
n **insulator**.
That will protect us from below...
...and this **holographic** safety shield will do the job from above!

insulator: a material that does not allow electric current to flow freely

holographic: created using laser lights

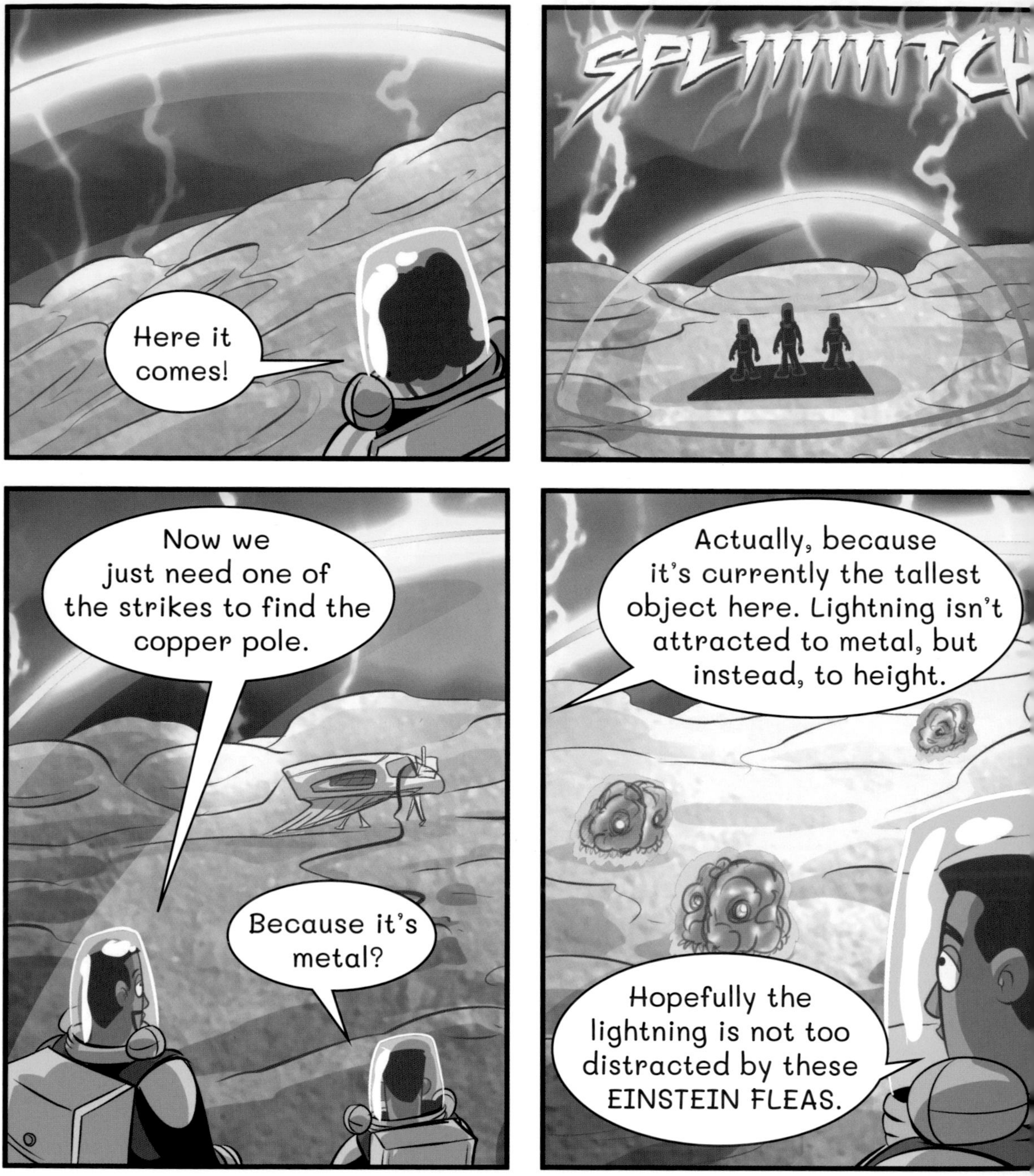
Here it comes!
SPLIIIIIITCH
Now we just need one of the strikes to find the copper pole.
Because it's metal?
Actually, because it's currently the tallest object here. Lightning isn't attracted to metal, but instead, to height.
Hopefully the lightning is not too distracted by these EINSTEIN FLEAS.

SCIENCE FACT

Albert Einstein was a physicist. He is thought of as one of the most influen scientists of all time. Following his de in 1955, a man by the name of Thoma Harvey stole his brain to study it.

THE FUNDAMENTALS OF ART

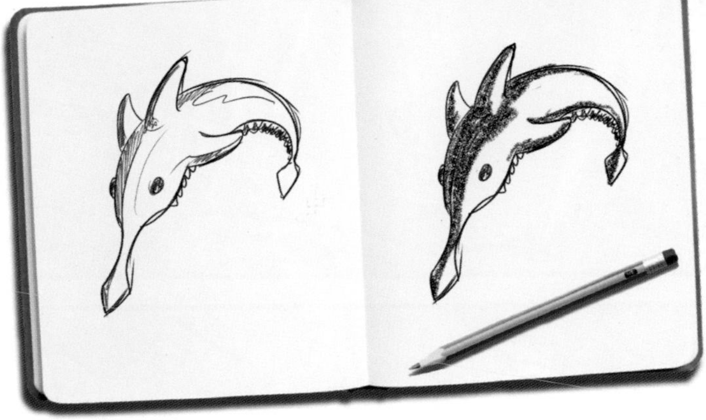

Let's put the FUN in the fundamentals of art by looking at texture. Texture is what gives art the impression of what an object would feel like. Review these 2 examples of Malcolm's imaginary dredge dolpheens. Notice how one looks smooth and one looks rough? That is texture.

- Art can impact all of our senses, not just our eyes.

- When you can imagine what something feels like, this is texture.

- Think of texture as the quality of an object's surface.

- Thinking about how something feels can impact our emotions. For example, if something looks slimy, it may gross us out, even though it is only a drawing!

- Artists use texture to bring out an emotional response from their audience.

- Don't just think of texture in terms of drawing or painting. Sculptors rely heavily on texture to express themselves.

- Take a look at the world around you. What textures can you see in everyday life? How would an object change if it felt differently?

ARTIST TIP: Try placing your paper on top of different surfaces while you draw or color to see what sorts of textures you can create. A sidewalk, carpet, or tile floor might give you some really fun results!

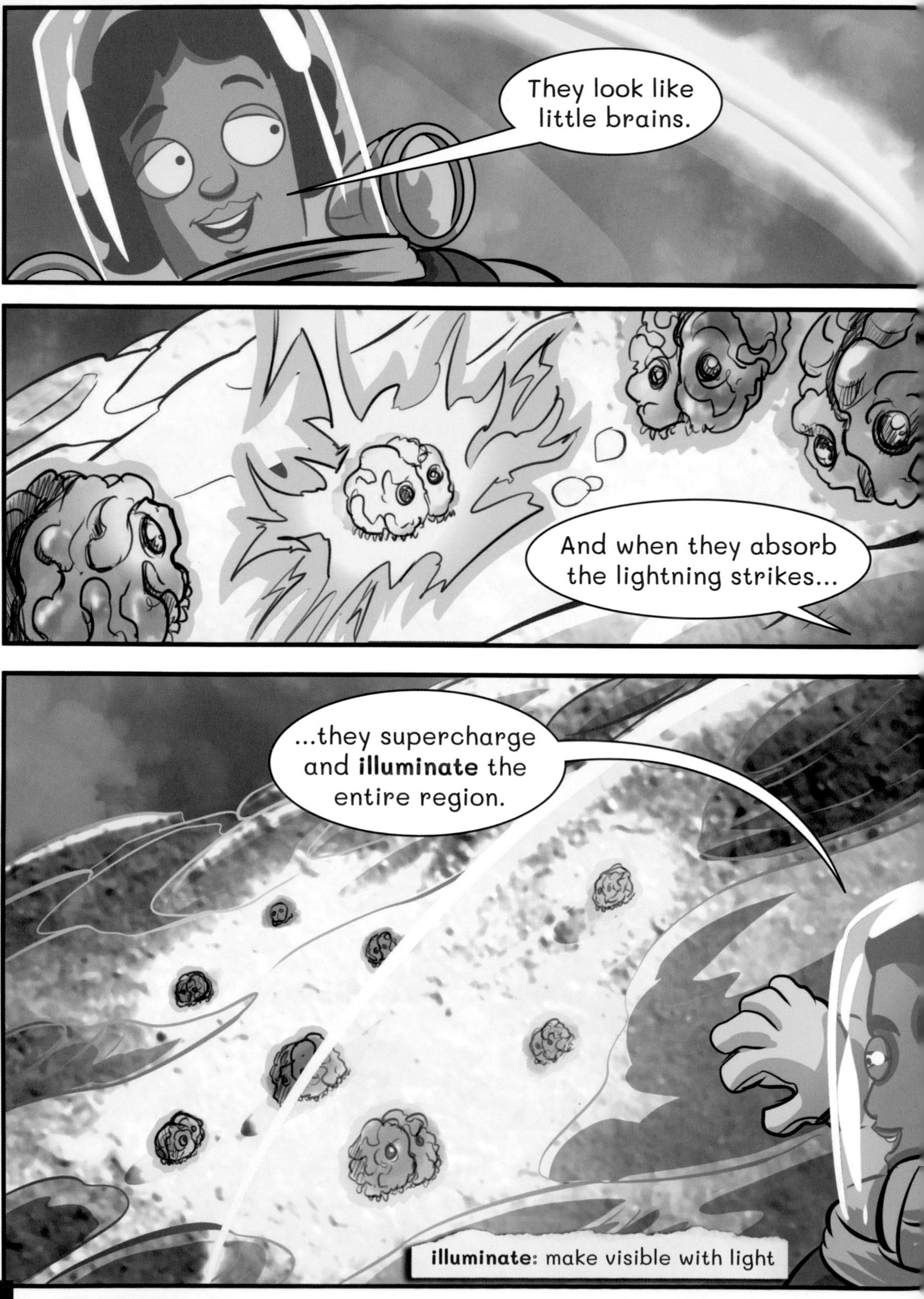
They look like little brains.
And when they absorb the lightning strikes...
...they supercharge and **illuminate** the entire region.
illuminate: make visible with light

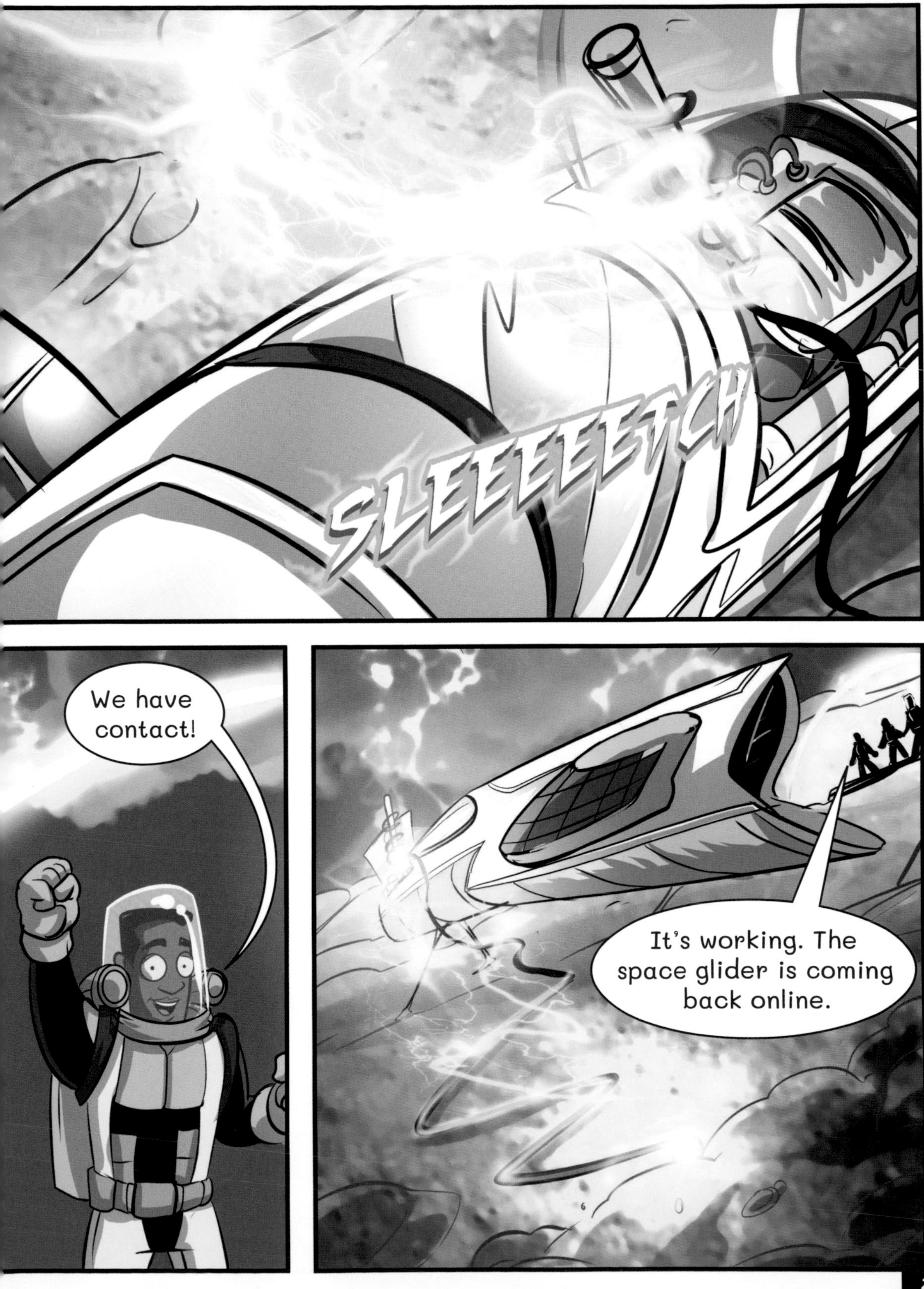
SLEEEEEETCH
We have contact!
It's working. The space glider is coming back online.

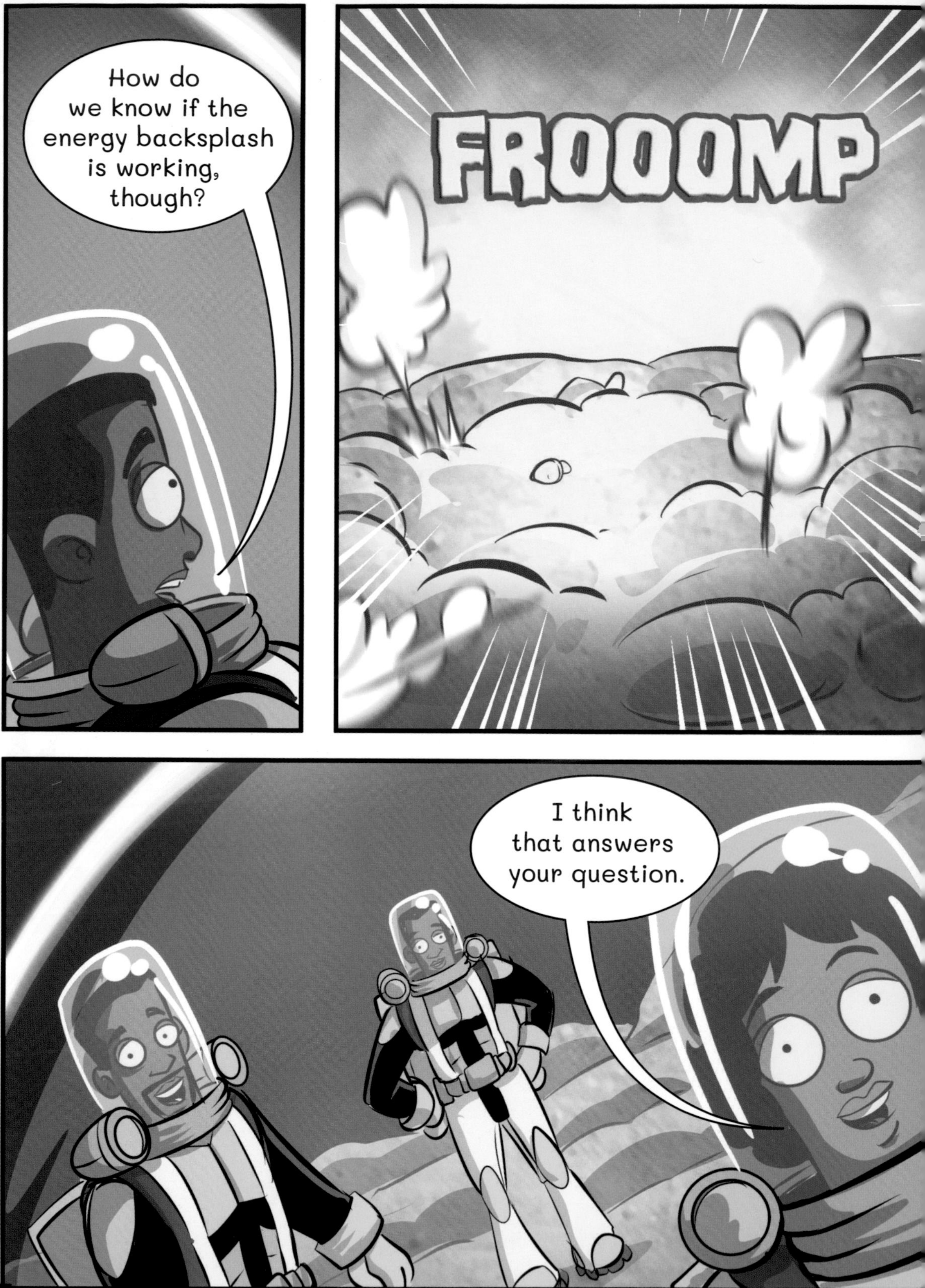
How do we know if the energy backsplash is working, though?
FROOOMP
I think that answers your question.

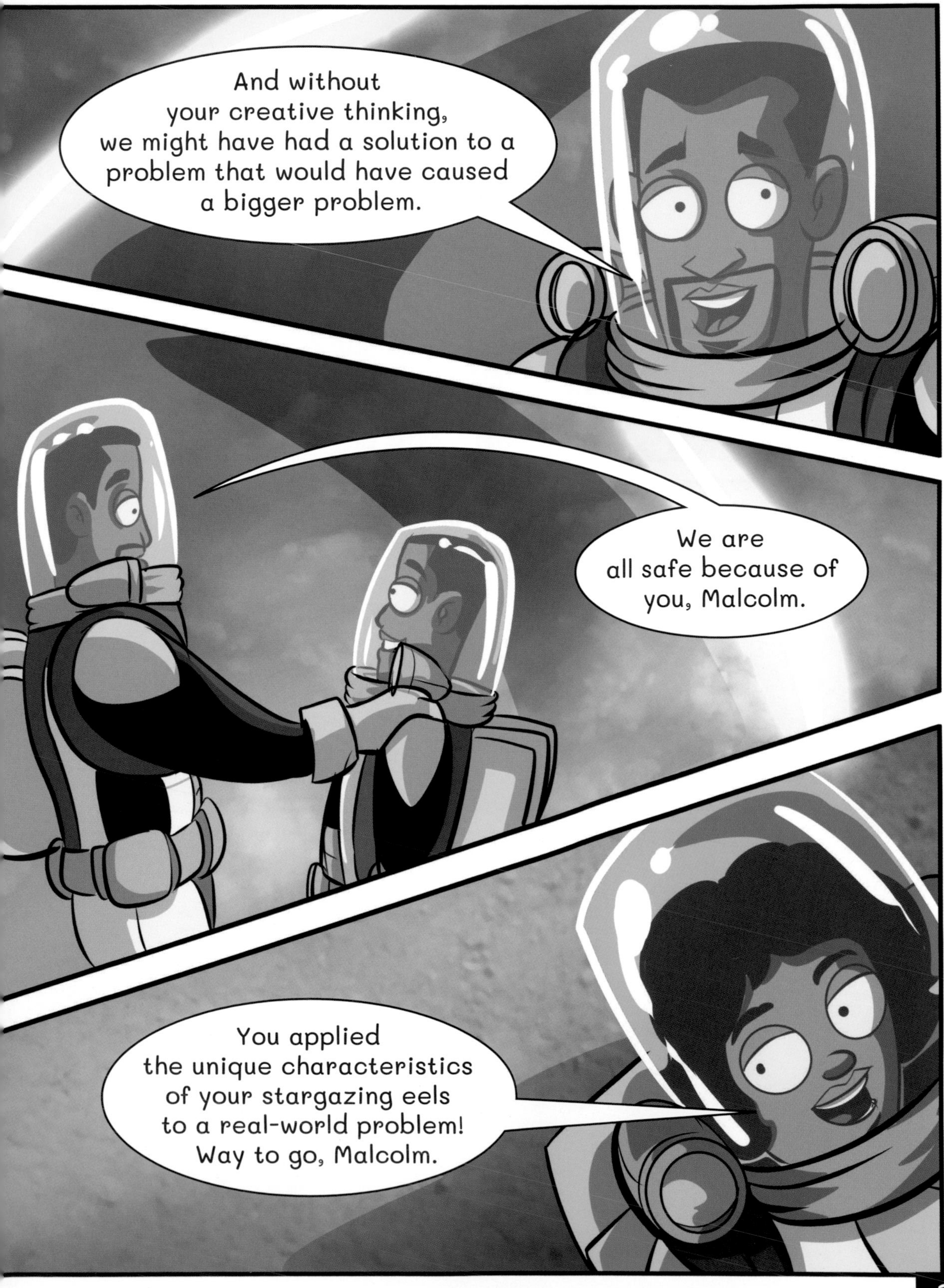
And without your creative thinking, we might have had a solution to a problem that would have caused a bigger problem.
We are all safe because of you, Malcolm.
You applied the unique characteristics of your stargazing eels to a real-world problem! Way to go, Malcolm.

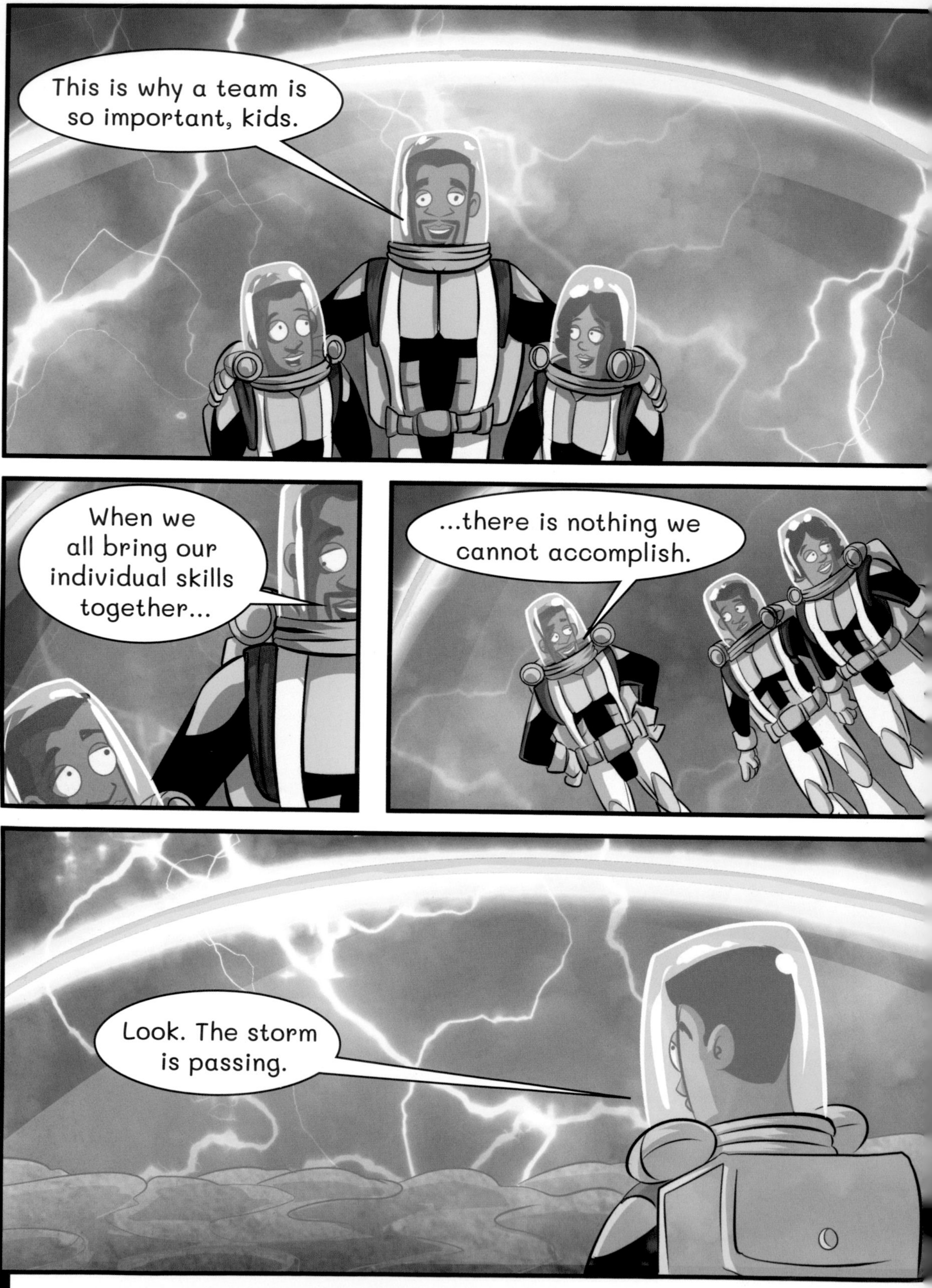
This is why a team is so important, kids.
When we all bring our individual skills together...
...there is nothing we cannot accomplish.
Look. The storm is passing.

MARS
SURVIVAL TIPS

There is a storm on the horizon, and you are out of your element in the elements. Don't panic. We have some tips to survive a lightning strike!

• The first step to safety is to avoid lightning completely. If you know a storm is coming, do not go outside.

• Sometimes, though, the weather catches you unexpectedly. Count to 30 if you see lightning. If you hear thunder before making it to the end, you need to seek shelter immediately. This is called the 30/30 rule.

• Not all shelters are created equal. Some structures, like sheds and baseball dugouts, may actually attract lightning.

• Buildings with wiring and plumbing will send any electrical charge away from the people inside.

• A vehicle offers protection as well. But roll up those windows!

• If there is no shelter, stay away from tall objects like trees and telephone poles. Lightning is drawn to the tallest objects in an area.

• Find a low area but do not lie flat. Doing so will cause more electricity to travel through the ground and into you.

• Crouch down, cover your ears with your hands, and place your head between your knees. This is the best way to minimize injury.

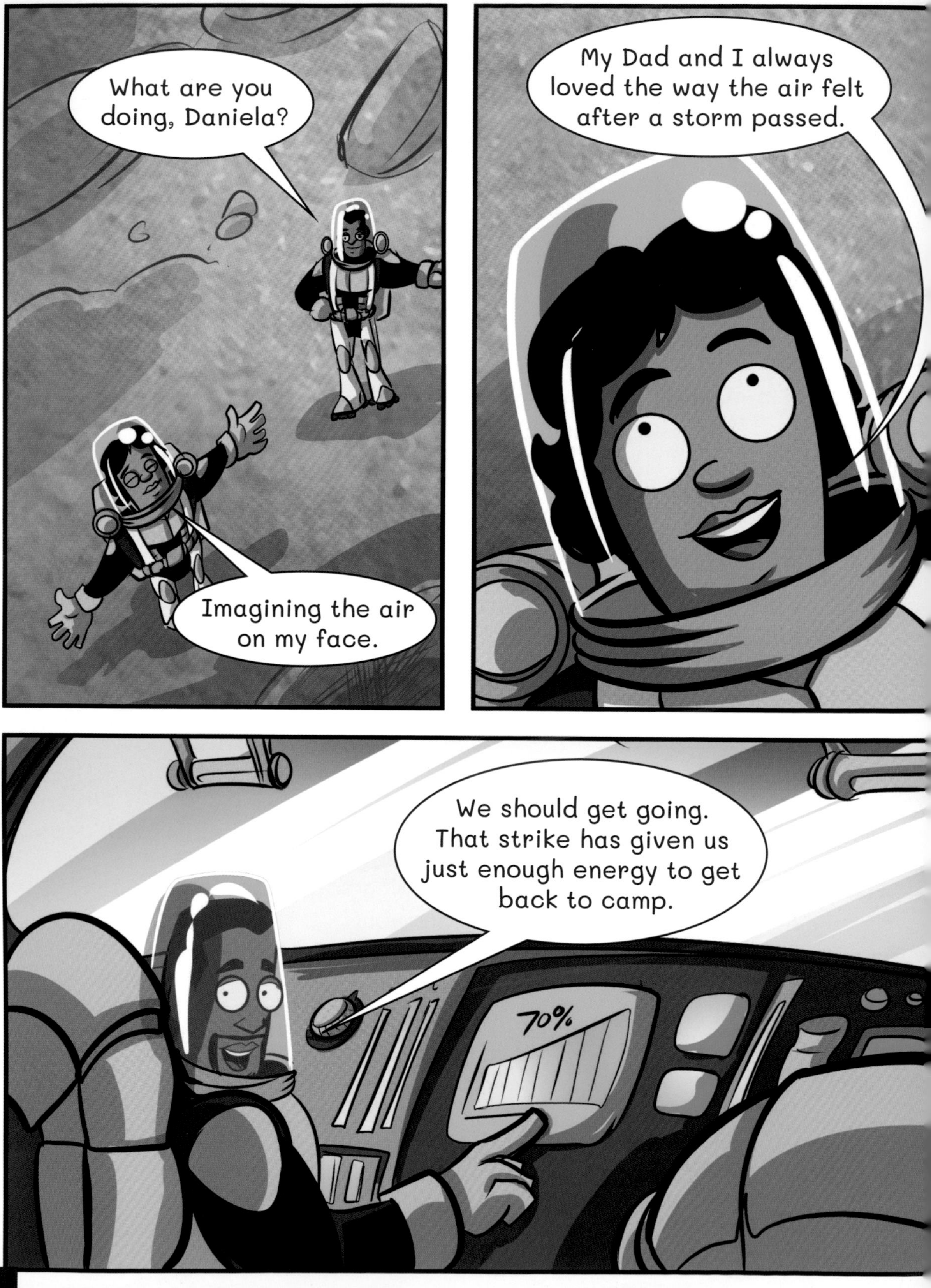
What are you doing, Daniela?
Imagining the air on my face.
My Dad and I always loved the way the air felt after a storm passed.
We should get going. That strike has given us just enough energy to get back to camp.
70%

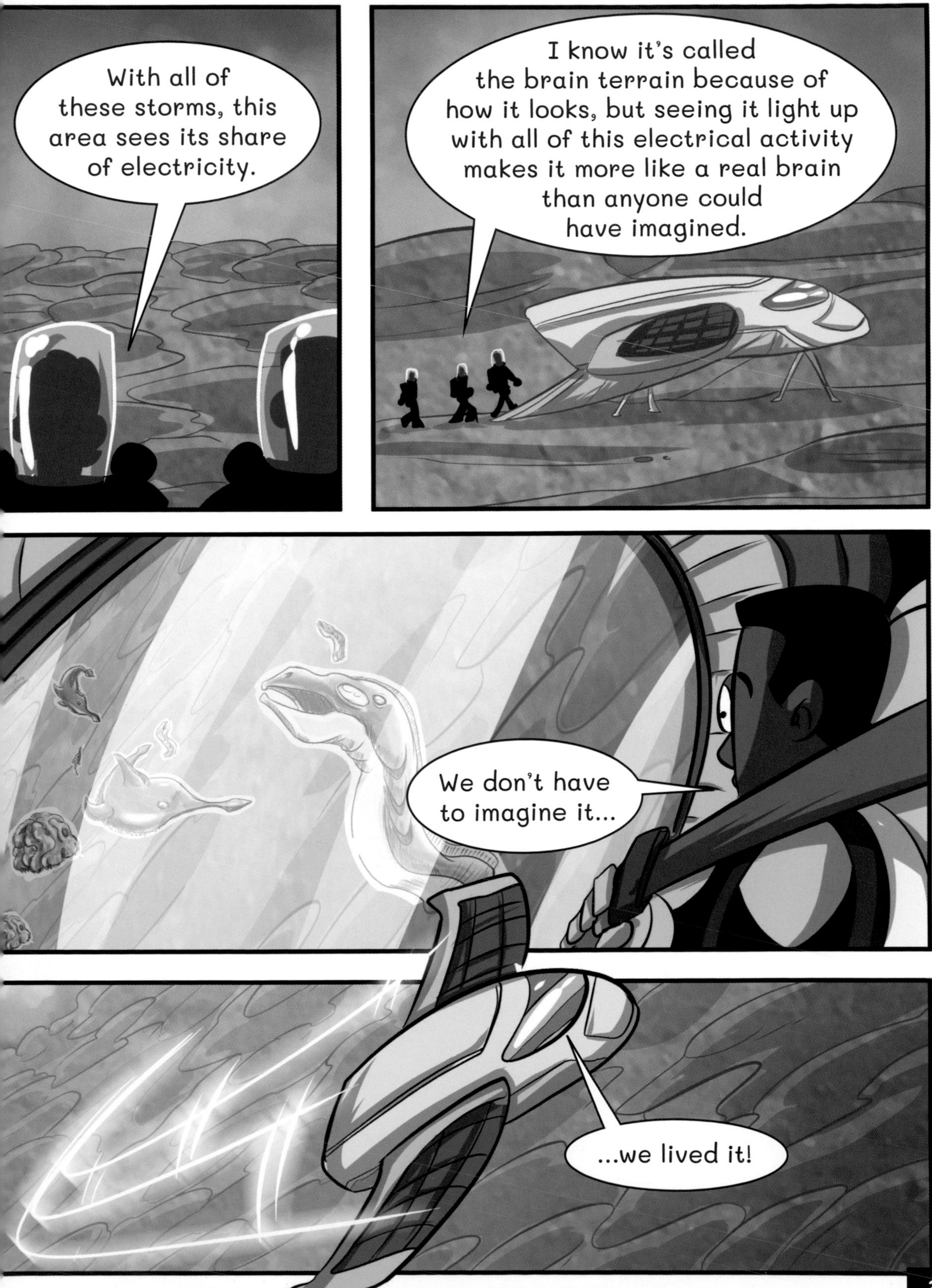

With all of these storms, this area sees its share of electricity.
I know it's called the brain terrain because of how it looks, but seeing it light up with all of this electrical activity makes it more like a real brain than anyone could have imagined.
We don't have to imagine it...
...we lived it!

DO-IT-YOURSELF LIGHTNING

Malcolm and the crew had to harness the power of lightning to recharge their vehicle. Did you know you can make your own lightning at home?

WHAT YOU NEED

- thumbtack
- aluminum pie pan
- pencil with an eraser
- styrofoam plate
- something made of wool, like a blanket

STEPS TO TAKE

1. With an adult's help, poke the thumbtack through the center of the pie pan. Attach the pencil to the pie pan by pushing the eraser onto the thumbtack.

2. Turn the plate upside down. Rub the bottom with the wool for a min or 2. Don't be afraid to rub hard!

3. Using the pencil like a handle, place the pie pan on top of the plate

4. Shut off the room lights.

5. Use your finger to touch the pie pan. What do you see? What do you feel?

SAFETY PAUSE

Tacks are sharp. Use only under adult supervision.

LEARN MORE

BOOKS

Bolte, Mari. *Preparing for Mars*. Ann Arbor, MI: Cherry Lake Publishing, 2022.

Vago, Mike. *The Planets are Very, Very, Very Far Away: A Journey Through the Amazing Scale of the Solar System*. New York, NY: The Experiment, 2021.

WEBSITES

Mission to Mars
https://kids.nationalgeographic.com/space/article/mission-to-mars

Get the facts on Mars, from the earliest discoveries to the latest news.

What is Mars?
https://www.nasa.gov/audience/forstudents/5-8/features/nasa-knows/what-is-mars-58.html

Facts, figures, and infographics with all the info on the Red Planet.

THE MARTIANS

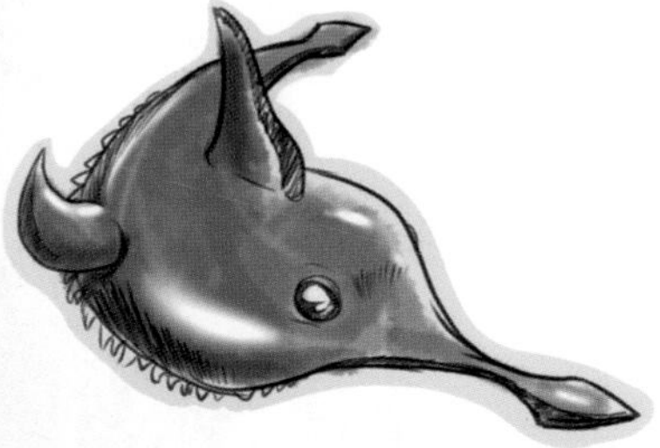

DREDGE DOLPHEENS

Part millipede and part dolphin, Malcolm crafts these inventive Martians to dive in an out of the Mars soil with their snouts shaped like shovels.

STARGAZING EELS

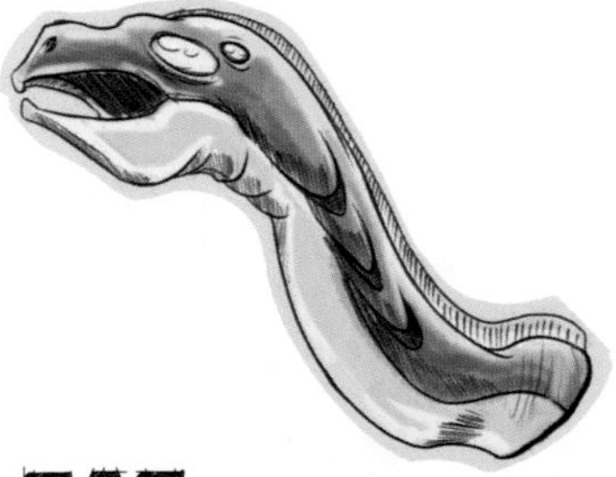

Malcolm sees these Martians rising out of the ground during electric storms and feeding on lightning.

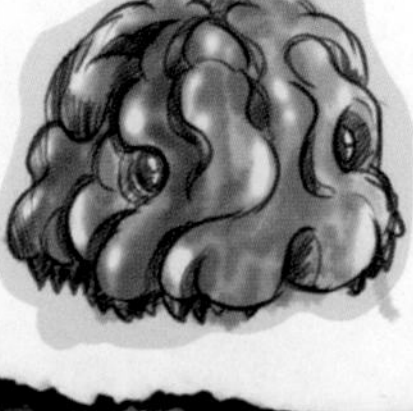

EINSTEIN FLEAS

Named after Albert Einstein, Malcolm draws these dog-sized Martians to resemble the human brain. They light the Mars landscape when struck by lightning.

GLOSSARY

analytically (ann-uh-LIH-tuk-lee) having a logical thought process

arthropods (ARE-thruh-pahdz) invertebrates with joined body parts, such as spiders, insects, and crustaceans

atmospheres (AT-muhs-feerz) layer of gas that surrounds planets

electrons (uh-LEK-trawnz) subatomic particles with negative charges

holographic (hol-uh-GRAF-ik) created using laser lights

illuminate (ill-OO-muh-nayt) make visible with light

inhabited (in-HA-buht-ed) occupied by living beings

insulator (IN-suh-lay-tuhr) a material that does not allow electric current to flow freely

plankton (PLAYNK-tuhn) tiny organisms found in water

solar cells (SOH-luhr SELS) devices that convert the sun's energy into electricit

voltage (VOL-tuhj) a measurement of electricity

INDEX